Junie B., First Grader
Toothless Wonder

Look for all of these great books by Barbara Park

Picture books
Psssst! It's Me . . . the Bogeyman

The Junie B. Jones series

BARBARA PARK

Junie B., First Grader Toothless Wonder

illustrated by Denise Brunkus

SCHOLASTIC INC.

New York   Toronto   London   Auckland   Sydney
Mexico City   New Delhi   Hong Kong   Buenos Aires

To Zachary Cheek . . . a great reader!

ISBN 0-439-56966-4

Text copyright © 2002 by Barbara Park. Illustrations copyright © 2002 by Denise Brunkus. All rights reserved. Published by Scholastic Inc., 557 Broadway, New York, NY 10012, by arrangement with Random House Children's Books, a division of Random House, Inc. SCHOLASTIC and associated logos are trademarks and/or registered trademarks of Scholastic Inc.

12 11 10 9 8 7 6 5 4 3 2 1   3 4 5 6 7 8/0

Printed in China

First Scholastic printing, September 2003

Contents

Contents

■ ■ ■ ■ ■ ■ ■ ■ ■ ■

Junie B., First Grader
Toothless Wonder

1

■ ■ ■ ■ ■ ■ ■ ■ ■ ■

Prizes

Friday

Dear first-grade journal,

Today we are having a ~~speeker~~ speaker in Room One. She is going to tell us all about ~~resikaling~~ recycling. Recycling is when you wash your trash, I believe.

Mr. Scary said to write in our journals till the speaker gets here. Only I don't even

feel like writing today. Because
I have a loose tooth, that's why.
And that thing is driving me
crazy.

Also, every time I write in
this journal I have to look up
words in the dumb ~~dikshunary~~ dictionary.
Except sometimes Mr. Scary
spells the words on the board
for us. And then I have to
cross out my mistakes. Plus
also, I erase holes in my
paper.

Spelling is not a ~~brees~~ breeze, I tell
you.

That is all I feel like writing

today. I am done with this
thing. And I mean it.
       From,
        Junie B., First Grader

I put down my pencil. And I opened my mouth. Then I reached in my finger and I wiggled my tooth.

That thing has been loose for a very long time. Only no matter how hard I wiggle it, it still won't come out.

I pulled on it a teensy bit.

"Ow, that hurt! You dumb bunny tooth!" I said.

May turned her head and looked at me.

May sits next to me in Room One.

She is not a pleasure.

"You shouldn't say *dumb bunny*, Junie

Jones," she said. "*Dumb bunny* is not a nice word."

I raised my eyebrows at her.

"Oh, really?" I said. "Well, thank you for telling me that, dumb bunny May."

Just then, May's face got puffy and red.

"DON'T SAY THAT WORD, I TOLD YOU!" she hollered.

My teacher stood up at his desk.

"Problem back there, girls?" he said.

"Yes, Mr. Scary!" said May. "There's *always* a problem back here. And her name is Junie Jones!"

I stamped my foot.

"*B.*, May!" I said. "B., B., B., B., B.! You're always forgetting my B.!"

Mr. Scary closed his eyes. "*Please*, girls. Can't we just have one morning without any spats?"

I looked surprised at that man.

"But I didn't even *spat,* Mr. Scary," I said. "My mother doesn't let me spat. Not even on the sidewalk."

After that, I went up to his desk. And I smiled very cute.

"I have a loose tooth," I said. "Would you like to see it, Mr. Scary? Huh? Would you?"

I opened my mouth and wiggled it for him.

"See it? See how loose it is? It is a loosey goosey, isn't it?" I said.

He smiled. "Wow. It really *is* loose, Junie B.," he said. "And it's a *top* tooth, too. Losing a top tooth is the best."

I looked puzzled.

"It is? How come it's the best, Mr. Scary?" I asked. "Is a top tooth funner than a bottom tooth, do you mean? Because last year I lost a bottom tooth. And I didn't actually get a kick out of it."

My teacher did a chuckle. "Ah . . . but when you lose a *top* tooth, your smile looks really cute, Junie B.," he said. "And when your new tooth comes in, you'll start looking like a *big* kid."

I did a gasp at that news.

"A big kid?" I said. "Really? I'm going to look like a big kid?"

Mr. Scary nodded. "Sure you are," he said. "Here. I'll show you what I mean."

He looked around the room. "Class? Does anyone in here have their big top teeth yet? If so, please raise your hand," he said.

All of the children looked and looked at each other.

But no one raised their hand.

Mr. Scary was surprised.

"Really?" he said. "No kidding? No one in our class has lost a top front tooth, huh?"

He turned around and shook my hand.

"Well, congratulations, Junie B. Jones," he said. "It looks like you're going to be the first person in Room One with a big top tooth!"

I felt very thrilled. "Thank you!" I said.

Then I skipped back to my seat. And I sat down real proud.

May did a huffy breath at me.

"Big deal. What's so special about losing a top tooth?" she said. "Everyone in our whole room is going to lose their top teeth, Junie Jones. It's not like you're the only one, you know."

I did a huffy breath right back at her.

"Yes, May. I know I'm not the *only* one," I said. "But I am the *first* one. And the *first* one is the winner. So there. Ha ha on you."

May crossed her arms. "Well, if you're the winner, then where's your prize? Huh, Junie Jones? I don't see a prize. Do you?"

I tapped my fingers kind of stumped. Then I hurried back to my teacher's desk again. And I patted him on the shoulder.

"Okay, here's the thing," I said. "The children are wondering where's my prize for being the tooth winner. And so how would you like to handle this situation?"

Mr. Scary did not answer right away.

Finally, he shrugged. "Well, the truth is, there *aren't* any prizes," he said. "I wasn't exactly running a contest, you know."

"Yes, I know," I said. "But I bet you could still come up with a little something to make me happy."

I pointed at his desk drawer.

"I bet there's something in there, probably," I said. "Teachers always have good stuff in their desk drawers, right? And so why don't we take a little look-see?"

Mr. Scary ran his fingers through his hair.

Then at last, he opened his drawer.

"Whoa! Is that a stapler I see there?" I said. "A stapler would be good, don't you think? I could really pound that thing, I bet. And so if you'll just hand it over, I will be on my way."

Mr. Scary shook his head. "No, Junie B.," he said. "No stapler."

I looked some more.

"Hey! Hold the phone!" I said. "Is that Tums I'm looking at?"

I leaned closer.

"Yes! Yes! It *is* Tums, Mr. Scary! You've got Tums just like my grampa Miller! And so I bet you suffer from gas and bloating. Am I correct?"

Mr. Scary quick closed the drawer.

Then he went to the supply closet and he got out a piece of shiny silver paper. And he scribbled a star.

He cut it out and pinned it on my shirt.

"There," he said. "That's your prize for your tooth, okay? You get to wear a shiny star for being the winner. Now please go back to your seat."

I looked down at my star.

"Yeah, only I don't actually think this is your best work," I said kind of quiet.

Mr. Scary pointed to my desk. He was not having a good morning, I think.

I went back and sat down.

May sneaked a peek at my star.

I tried to act proud of it.

"Well, well, well. What do you know . . . a *prize*," I said.

May did a mad breath and quick turned away.

I looked down at my star again.

This time it looked prettier, I think.

2

Uncle Lou

The speaker came at ten o'clock.

Her name was Miss Chris.

Miss Chris told us all about recycling.

Also, she showed us a movie.

It was called *Dan, Dan the Soda Can.*

It was very thrilling, I tell you. 'Cause Dan, Dan the Soda Can lived in a soda machine at a gas station. Then one day, a lady bought him to drink. Only too bad for Dan, Dan. 'Cause after the lady drank his soda, she threw him right out her car window. And Dan, Dan got his can all dented.

But hurray, hurray! A cop saw the lady littering. And he gave her a big fat ticket!

Then a can man took Dan, Dan to a recycling center. And the man got cash money. Plus Dan, Dan got fixed up good as new. And bingo! He turned into Dan, Dan the *Orange Juice* Can!

It was a miracle, I tell you!

Room One clapped and clapped at that happy ending.

Then Miss Chris passed around stickers of Dan, Dan the Soda Can for us to stick to our shirts. And the stickers said RECYCLING MAKES CENTS. Ha! Get it?

Cents sounds like *sense*! And that is a good one, I think!

After that, all of us went to lunch and recess. And we were still in happy moods.

On the playground, José and Lennie and Shirley asked to see my loose tooth. Then pretty soon, the other children wanted to see it, too.

And so finally, I stood them all in a row. And I let them look real close.

After they looked, I walked down the row. And I showed them how far I could bend it.

Herb clapped and clapped.

José and Lennie whistled.

Sheldon tried to pick me up.

That is not a normal reaction, I think.

"You're going to look cool when it finally comes out, Junie B.," said Herb.

"Sí," said José. "You're going to look *really* cool. Like a hockey player, I bet."

"Yeah," said Lennie. "Hockey players almost never have any teeth."

"Neither do kick-boxers," said Shirley. "Maybe you'll look like a kick-boxer, Junie B."

Just then, Sheldon did a sigh. "I just hope you don't look like my toothless uncle Lou," he said. "My toothless uncle Lou never brushed or flossed. And then all his teeth fell out."

I made a sick face.

Sheldon shrugged. "Well, it's not like he's *totally* toothless," he said. "He still has one bottom tooth left. It's kind of yellow. But it still can bite an apple."

After that, Sheldon walked away.

I watched him go.

Then I sat down in the grass.

And I tried and tried not to think of toothless Uncle Lou.

After school, me and Herb rode the bus home together.

We sit with each other every single day. Except not on Saturdays or Sundays or weekends.

Me and Herb talk about lots of stuff on the bus. Only today I didn't feel like talking, hardly. 'Cause I was still upset about looking like Uncle you-know-who.

I slumped down in my seat very glum.

"What if I look like a weirdo?" I said. "Huh, Herb? What if I look like toothless Uncle Lou?"

Herbert patted me. "Don't worry. You won't . . . probably."

I kept on worrying.

"Yeah, only today is Friday, Herb," I said. "And so by Monday my tooth will already be out, I bet. And so what if I come to school looking like toothless Uncle Lou? And then all of Room One starts making fun of me? And they form a circle around me, and they laugh and skip and throw fruit?"

Then, all of a sudden, I did a gasp. 'Cause an even *worser* problem popped in my head.

I grabbed Herb's shirt.

"Oh, no, Herb! Oh, no!" I said. "What if I don't even *look* like myself on Monday! Not even a tiny bit, I mean! And then I get on this bus. And you don't even recognize me. And so you pass right by my seat. And then I have to sit by myself.

All alone . . . and toothless."

Herb looked down at his shirt.

He said to please take my hands off of him.

He smoothed himself out.

"Maybe you should look on the bright side, Junie B.," he said. "Even if all of that bad stuff happens—which it won't, probably—you'll still end up with a bunch of money from the tooth fairy. Right? And that's good, isn't it?"

As soon as he said that, chill bumps came on my skin. And my stomach got flutterflies in it.

I quick looked out the window so Herb couldn't see my face.

'Cause guess what?

The tooth fairy is a whole other can of worms.

3

■ ■ ■ ■ ■ ■ ■ ■ ■

Ow!

I walked home from my bus stop very slow.

Walking is good for thinking, I think.

Talking is good for thinking, too.

"I just wish I wasn't the *first* one, that's all," I said out loud to myself. "I wish the other children in Room One were losing their teeth, too. Then all of us would look toothless together. And no one would throw fruit."

I did a big breath at me.

"Yeah, only that is the dumbest thing I ever heard of," I said. "'Cause you can't make other children have loose teeth, Junie B."

I rolled my eyes.

"Yeah, only I already *know* that, Junie B.," I said. "But I really don't want to be first. And so why can't my tooth just stay in my mouth a little longer? That's what I would like to know."

I crossed my arms at myself.

"'Cause you keep *wiggling* it, that's why," I said. "Maybe if you didn't wiggle it, it would get tight again. Did you ever think of that? Huh? Did you?"

I walked and walked some more.

Then, all of a sudden, I did a gasp.

'Cause I *did* think of that! Ha!

I ran to my house speedy quick.

My grampa Frank Miller was baby-sitting my fussy brother named Ollie.

"Grampa Miller! I know what to do about my tooth! I know what to do about my tooth!" I hollered real happy.

Grampa Miller was bouncing Ollie on his lap.

Ollie was wearing his drool bib. Also, he was slobbering and chewing on his arm.

Ollie will not be popular in school, probably.

Mother says he is drooly and fussy because he will be getting teeth soon.

She is kidding herself, I think.

Just then, Ollie started to cry.

Grampa Miller looked weary of that boy.

I took Ollie away from him.

"Don't worry, Grampa. I know how to calm this baby down," I said.

After that, I patted Ollie's back very nice.

Then I hummed real soft in his ear.

And I put him in the hall closet.

Grampa quick got him out of there.

He put Ollie in his playpen. And he gave him animal crackers.

Animal crackers are crackers that make babies stop crying.

Also, I enjoy an occasional cracker myself.

After Ollie stopped fussing, Grampa Miller came back in the kitchen. And he put me on his lap.

"Okay, little girl. I'm ready to listen to your news now," he said. "What were you saying about your tooth? Did it get any looser at school today?"

I clapped my hands together.

"That's what I was going to tell you about, Grampa!" I said. "'Cause at school I found out that I am the first person in Room One to lose a top front tooth. And so at first I felt proud about that news. Only then I got nervous. On account of who wants to look like toothless Uncle Lou, that's why. And so then I had a long talk with myself. And hurray, hurray! I decided not to lose my tooth after all!"

My grampa raised his eyebrows at me.

"Really?" he said. "You're not going to lose your tooth, huh? Do you really think you can do that, honey?"

"Yes!" I said. "I know I can do it, Grampa. 'Cause all I have to do is not wiggle it anymore. And then it will get real tight in my mouth again! I am *sure* of it! I'm positive."

I reached in my mouth and touched my tooth very light with my finger.

"Yup!" I said. "I can feel it! It's tighter already!"

I opened my mouth and pointed. "See it, Grampa? See how tight it's getting?"

Grampa Miller squinted his eyes. "Gee, honey, I don't know," he said. "It still looks pretty loose to me."

Then—without even asking—he reached in my mouth. And he started to *wiggle* it.

"No!" I yelled. "No! No! No!"

I snapped my mouth shut.

"OW!" said my grampa.

He quick pulled out his finger.

"OW!" I said right back.

'Cause I felt a pinch, that's why!

I poked all around with my tongue.

Something did not feel right in there.

My heart started to pound very fast.

I held my breath.

Then I opened my mouth kind of sickish.

And I spit my tooth right into my hand.

4

Freako

I ran and ran all over the house.

"OH, NO!" I shouted. "OH, NO! OH, NO! MY GRAMPA FRANK MILLER KNOCKED MY TOOTH OUT! MY GRAMPA FRANK MILLER KNOCKED MY TOOTH OUT!"

Grampa ran after me.

"No, I didn't. Of *course* I didn't, Junie B.," he said. "Your tooth came out when you bit down on my finger."

I kept running and shouting.

"I LOOK LIKE UNCLE LOU! I LOOK

LIKE UNCLE LOU! HELP! HELP! HELP! I LOOK LIKE UNCLE LOU!"

I zoomed to the front door and opened it wide.

"911! 911! MY TOOTH'S KNOCKED OUT! MY TOOTH'S KNOCKED OUT!"

Grampa quick picked me up and carried me back inside.

Then he took me to the bathroom. And he gave me a paper cup with water.

"Rinse and spit," he said.

I did what he said.

Only that's when the worstest thing of all happened.

'Cause my spit water turned *pink*!

I did a gasp at that sight.

"BLOOD! BLOOD! THERE'S BLOOD IN MY SPIT!" I hollered some more.

Grampa Miller covered his ears. "*Please,* Junie B. Just stop the screeching."

After that, he took an aspirin. Plus also, he ate two Tums.

I kept on rinsing and spitting.

Then finally, my spit water turned regular.

"Whew," I said. "That was a close one. I was almost out of blood."

Grampa bent down next to me and smiled. "Well, let's have a look," he said.

I opened my mouth for him.

He looked in and did a chuckle.

Then he lifted me up to the mirror so I could see, too.

I quick closed my mouth again. 'Cause I was nervous to see myself, of course.

My tongue felt my tooth hole. It felt very roomy in there.

"Well?" said Grampa Miller. "Aren't you going to look, honey? It looks cute, Junie B. It really does."

My heart pounded and pounded.

Then—fast as a wink—I opened my lips. And I did a little peek at my mouth.

I quick closed my eyes again.

'Cause what do you know?

A freako.

"Put me down, Grampa," I said. "Put me down right now. I don't want to look at myself again. I don't, I don't, I don't."

Grampa Miller put me down.

Just then, my nose started to sniffle very much. And my eyes got tears in them.

"I *hate* me," I said. "I hate the way I look."

Grampa blew my nose on toilet paper.

"I'm never going to look at myself again," I said. "Not ever, ever, *never*! And I *mean* it."

Grampa bent down next to me again.

"I want you to listen to me, little girl," he said. "I would never lie to you, Junie B. You look every bit as cute without your tooth as you did with it."

He gave me a hug. "Your new smile is wonderful," he said. "You didn't even give it a chance, honey. You really need to look at it again. Honest you do."

He ruffled my hair. "Do it for me, okay? Just give yourself one more chance."

I rocked back and forth on my feet very slow. 'Cause I needed to think this over, that's why.

Finally, I did a big breath. "Oh, okay, Grampa," I said. "If you really want to lift me up there again, I guess I will let you. But I'm only doing this to be nice."

Grampa Miller patted my head. "You're very kind," he said.

After that, he lifted me back up to the mirror.

Very slow, I opened my mouth again. And I peeked at my new tooth hole.

"Try smiling," said my grampa. "You'll love your new smile. I know you will."

I did a nervous breath. Then I smiled at myself kind of shy.

"See?" said Grampa Miller. "See how cute it looks?"

I didn't answer him. Instead, I made another face at myself. And then another one. And another one.

Pretty soon, I tried every face in the book.

Finally, Grampa winked at me.

"So what do you think, little girl?" he said. "Hmm? How do you think you look?"

I smiled kind of shy again.

"I think I look fascinating, Frank," I said.

Grampa Miller put me back on the floor.

Then he went to the kitchen. And he got a stool. And he brought it back to the bathroom.

He helped me up to the top step.

I stared at myself till Mother came home.

5

The Fairy

That night we had festivities.

Festivities is when my grampa and grandma come over. And all of us eat cake.

Grandma Helen Miller made the cake herself. She put a big smiley face on the top. Only that is not all. 'Cause the smiley face had a tooth missing! Just like me!

I laughed and laughed at that silly thing. Then I reached in my pocket. And I got my tooth. And I passed it all around the table.

"Oh, that's a *beaut*, Junie B.," said Grandma Miller.

"I know it, Grandma. I know it is a beaut," I said real proud. "I can't wait to take it to school for Show-and-Tell. The children are going to love this thing."

Daddy looked strange at me.

"Oh, gee . . . I don't know, honey," he said. "I'm not really sure you should take your tooth to school."

Mother shook her head.

"No, Junie B. That's *definitely* not a good idea," she said. "And besides, you won't even have your tooth on Monday, remember? You have to leave it for the tooth fairy tonight."

Just then, my skin got chill bumps again. And the flutterflies came back in my stomach.

'Cause I know stuff about the fairy, that's why.

My voice felt kind of shaky.

"Yeah, only what if I don't want to leave my tooth for the fairy, Mother?" I said. "What if I just want to take it to Show-and-Tell, and that's all?"

Mother shook her head again. "No, Junie B. No Show-and-Tell," she said. "Taking a tooth to Show-and-Tell is just . . . well, it's just—"

"Disgusting," said Daddy.

"Yes," said Mother. "Disgusting."

I whined at those two. "No, it isn't," I said. "Lots of kids bring teeth to school. 'Cause one time Roger brought a shark's tooth. And he even let me and Herb put it right in our mouths. And then we looked like sharks, too."

I thought some more.

"Plus another time, Shirley brought her

grandmother's dentures. And lots of us put those in our mouths, too."

Grandma Miller did a little gag. Only I don't actually know why.

My grampa patted her hand. "Just be glad she doesn't want to take the spit cup," he whispered.

Just then, my whole face lighted up. 'Cause I have ears like a hawk, of course!

"The spit cup! The spit cup! I will take the spit cup!" I hollered.

I jumped down from my chair. And I zoomed to the bathroom.

Then I got the spit cup out of the trash. And I dusted it off real good.

"Good news, people!" I shouted real loud. "There's still some blood around the edges!"

I quick ran back to show them.

Grandma Miller closed her eyes at that sight.

Then Mother put her head on the table and hid her face in her arms.

The festivities were over, I believe.

After Grandma and Grampa Miller left, Mother took me into the bathroom. And we brushed my teeth real careful.

Then I took my loose tooth out of my pocket. And I brushed that guy, too.

I held it up to the light. "Look," I said. "Look how shiny I made it. I really wish I could take this tooth to school, Mother. I really, really wish that with all my might."

Mother gave me a hug. "I know you do, Junie B.," she said. "But it's still going to be fun to put it under your pillow tonight, isn't it?"

She smiled. "I remember when I was a little girl. I couldn't *wait* to wake up in the morning and find out how much money the tooth fairy had left me."

My skin got prickly at that name again.

Also, sweaty came on my head.

I thought and thought about what to do.

Then finally, I stood on my tiptoes. And I whispered in Mother's ear.

"Yeah, only I know stuff about the fairy, Mother," I said. "I know the *truth*."

Mother looked shocked at me.

"The truth?" she said. "You know the truth?"

"Yes," I whispered again. "I know the *exact* truth, Mother. 'Cause last year Paulie Allen Puffer told me the whole entire story."

I took another big breath. Then I cupped

my hands around her ear. And I talked even
quieter.

"The fairy isn't *real*," I said. "The tooth
fairy is just *pretend*."

Mother's eyes got big and wide at me.

"No!" she said.

"*Yes*," I whispered back. "Paulie Allen
learned it from his big brother. The tooth

fairy isn't a fairy at all. She's actually a teensy little tooth witch."

Mother's mouth came all the way open. "A tooth *witch*?"

"Shh!" I said. "We have to talk soft, Mother. If the tooth witch hears anyone telling her secret, she flies into their room at night. And she pinches their cheeks."

Mother covered her face with her hands.

She was in shock, I believe.

"Paulie Allen's brother even *saw* the tooth witch," I said. "'Cause one night he put a tooth under his pillow. And then he stayed awake all night. And he saw the tooth witch fly into his room on a teensy little toothbrush."

"Oh, my," said Mother.

"I know it is *oh, my*," I said. "And that is not even the worstest part. 'Cause the witch walked right under his pillow. And she carried out his tooth. And then she chomped a big bite out of it. Just like it was a little tooth apple."

Mother made a noise behind her hands.

I patted her very nice. "I know how you feel," I said. "This is very hard to hear."

Finally, Mother took her hands away.

"But it doesn't really make sense, Junie B.," she said. "I mean, why would a mean little witch leave *money* under the pillow? A witch would never do something that nice, would she?"

I rolled my eyes way up to the ceiling. 'Cause sometimes I have to explain *everything* to that woman.

"Of *course* she would, Mother. Don't you get it? The witch leaves money so that children think she's really a fairy. 'Cause if children don't think there's a fairy, they won't leave their teeth. Right? And if they don't leave their teeth, the witch won't get any tooth apples."

Mother closed her eyes very tight.

Then, all of a sudden, she opened up the bathroom door.

And she ran right out of the room.

She was taking it harder than I thought.

6

Full of Soup

That night, Daddy tucked me into bed.

He said that Paulie Allen Puffer's brother is full of soup.

"There's no such thing as a tooth witch, Junie B.," he said. "I promise you there isn't. Paulie Allen Puffer's brother just made that up to scare Paulie Allen. And then Paulie Allen said it to scare you, too."

I shook my head. "No, Daddy. No. It's not made up. I know it isn't. 'Cause the tooth witch makes *sense*, that's why," I said. "She makes *way* more sense than a fairy."

Daddy raised his eyebrows.

"Why?" he asked. "Why does a witch make more sense than a fairy?"

"*Because,*" I said. "Because the tooth witch likes to *chomp* the teeth. But the tooth fairy doesn't do anything with the teeth at all, right? And so why would she even pay money for them?"

Daddy did a little frown.

"Well, I don't know, exactly," he said. "But I'm sure that she must do *something* with the teeth, Junie B. There are other things to do with teeth besides just chomping them, you know."

"Like what?" I asked.

Daddy put his head in his hands. Then he thought and thought and thought.

After he got done thinking, he went to get Mother.

She came into my room carrying fussy Ollie.

She handed him to Daddy and sat down on my bed.

"Daddy said you have another problem about the tooth fairy," she said.

I nodded.

"Yes," I said. "'Cause if there's really a fairy, then she has to have a reason to want the teeth. Right, Mother? She wouldn't just

throw them in the garbage. 'Cause that doesn't make any sense. Plus also, it would hurt my feelings."

Mother hugged me.

"No, Junie B. Of *course* she doesn't throw them in the garbage," she said. "I'm sure the fairy does something very special with the teeth."

"Like what?" I said.

Mother ran her tired fingers through her

hair. She stood up and walked back and forth on my rug.

Then, all of a sudden, her face got brighter.

"*I* know. I bet the fairy uses the teeth to make *jewelry*," she said.

At first, Daddy and I didn't say any words. We just stared and stared at that woman.

"Jewelry?" I said finally.

Mother smiled. "Yes, of *course*," she said. "She probably uses the teeth to make little tooth necklaces and bracelets and cute little toe rings. How does that sound?"

I made a sick face.

"It sounds repulsive," said Daddy.

Mother stopped smiling.

She quick took Ollie back from Daddy. And she hurried out of my room.

After she left, Daddy finished tucking me in bed.

"I'm sorry about that, Junie B.," he said. "I'm afraid Ollie has your mother worn to a frazzle these days. But I'm sure she's not right about that jewelry thing."

He did a little shiver.

"No. Certainly she's not," he said.

Then—before I could ask any more questions about the fairy—he kissed me good night. And he rushed out of my room as fast as Mother.

That night, I did not put my tooth under my pillow.

Also, I did not put it under there the night after that. Or the night after that.

Because what do you know . . .

The fairy still did not make sense.

7

A Stumper

The next morning was school.

I put my spit cup into my backpack. And I took it to my bus stop. 'Cause Mother said I couldn't take my tooth. But the spit cup was Grampa's idea.

I saved Herb a seat. Then I bounced up and down real excited. 'Cause I couldn't wait for him to see me, of course!

Finally, we got to his bus stop.

I waved to him from the window.

Then, ha! I leaned my face real close to the glass. And I smiled my biggest smile!

Herb's eyeballs popped out of his head!

He ran on the bus zippedy quick.

"It came out, Herb! It came out!" I said. "My tooth came out on Friday! And it's been out ever since!"

I smiled for him again.

"See me, Herb? See how I look? I look fascinating, right? I don't look like Uncle Lou, hardly."

Herb's eyeballs kept popping out at me.

"Whoa!" he said. "Wow!"

I laughed at that nice comment.

I smiled and pointed.

"See my tooth hole, Herb? Huh? I look cute, right? I don't even look like Uncle Lou! Correct?"

Herb said *Wow* again.

After that, I quick got my backpack. And I unzipped the zipper.

"Yeah, only wait till you see *this*, Herbert!" I said. "I brought something special for you to see!"

After that, I pulled out the cup. And I put it right on his lap.

"Ta-daaa! It's my *spit* cup, Herb! I used this cup to rinse my actual spit!"

I showed him the edges. "See the pink color right there? That pink is from the bleeding."

Herbert's face did not look delighted.

"Okay. Thank you," he said. "Please get it off of me now."

I got it off.

"But I thought you would like this," I said very disappointed.

Herb patted me. "Live and learn," he said.

Pretty soon, his face got normal again.

"So how much money did you get from the fairy, Junie B.?" he asked. "Did you get a lot of cash?"

My stomach did a flip-flop at that question.

'Cause I didn't want to discuss that matter, of course.

I squirmed in my seat kind of worried. Then I looked out the window. And I didn't talk.

Herb tapped on me.

"What's wrong, Junie B.?" he said. "How come you're not answering me? The fairy did come, right? She didn't forget you, did she?"

I looked all around. Then I scooted next to him very close. And I quieted my voice to a whisper.

"Yeah, only I can't even discuss that matter, Herb," I said. "'Cause I know stuff about that fairy."

"Stuff? What kind of stuff?" he asked.

I whispered even softer.

"Sorry," I said. "But I have to keep it a secret. And so please don't ask me any more questions. And I mean it."

After that, I pretended to lock my lips. And I threw away the key.

I saw that on TV once.

Herb looked annoyed at me.

I unlocked my lips again.

"Don't be mad at me," I said. "I can't help what I know, Herb. And anyway, all you have to do is think about it. 'Cause the fairy doesn't make sense."

Herb scratched his head. "What do you mean she doesn't make sense? Why doesn't she?"

I crossed my arms.

"Because what does the fairy do with the teeth, Herbert? Huh? Did you ever ask yourself that problem? Why would a fairy pay money for teeth when she doesn't even use them? It sounds kind of fishy, don't you think?"

Herb just stared at me.

"Well?" I said. "Do you know the answer, Herb? A fairy wouldn't just throw the teeth in the garbage, would she? 'Cause that doesn't even add up. Only nobody knows *what* she does with them, apparently. Not even you, I bet."

Herb wrinkled his eyebrows.

"I never thought about it," he said.

He tapped on his chin. "What does the fairy do with the teeth? Hmm . . . that's a stumper, all right."

After that, he slid way down in his seat. And he thought and thought some more.

I thought some more, too.

We rode to school real quiet.

8

Smiling

When we finally got to school, I started feeling shaky inside.

'Cause I didn't want to get laughed at, remember? Plus I was still concerned about the fruit throwing.

I closed my mouth real tight. And I walked back to my desk.

Lennie smiled and waved at me.

I waved back. Then, very slow, I did a shy smile.

That's when Lennie jumped up from his desk. And he did a loud whoop!

"Cool!" he said. "You look cool, Junie B.!"

José heard Lennie and came to see. Then he grinned and grinned at my brand-new smile. And he gave me a happy high five.

And that is not even the *best* part!

Because Mr. Scary saw what was going on. And he came all the way to my desk to see my tooth. And he gave me a smiley-face sticker!

After that, he clapped his hands together. And he made a 'nouncement to Room One.

He told them I lost my tooth. And he
asked me to stand up and show them my
special new smile.

I swallowed real nervous.

Then I stood up kind of jittery. And I
opened my lips a teensy bit so the children
could see my tooth hole.

And what do you know?

Room One was happy for me!

All of them smiled real nice.

Except, not May, of course.

May just rolled her eyeballs.

"I think you look weird, Junie Jones," she said. "I think your smile looks silly."

I sat down. "No, May. *This* is a silly smile," I said.

Then I put my fingers in the sides of my mouth. And I stretched my smile across my face. And I wiggled my tongue at her very fast.

Lennie and José laughed and laughed.

And guess what? At lunchtime, I made my smile even funnier. 'Cause Lennie gave me a raisin. And I put it right in my tooth hole! And it stuck there very hilarious!

Shirley laughed her head off at that joke.

I am beginning to enjoy that girl.

"So how much did the tooth fairy leave you?" she asked. "Did you get a bundle?"

"Yeah," said Lennie. "I was wondering that, too."

I started feeling squirmy again. I looked at Herb kind of worried.

He tried to explain the matter to them.

"Well, uh . . . Junie B. didn't exactly leave her tooth for the fairy yet," he said.

All of the children looked at me. "Why?" they said. "Why didn't you leave it, Junie B.?"

I squirmed some more. Then finally, I took a deep breath.

"I've got *issues* with that fairy, that's why," I said kind of quiet.

"Issues?" asked Lennie. "Like what kind of issues?"

I swallowed real hard. "Issues like . . . well, you know . . . like what does she do with the teeth, for instance," I said.

For a minute, nobody said anything.

Then May made the cuckoo sign at me.

"What does the fairy do with the teeth?" she said. "What kind of dumb issue is that?"

I flashed my angry eyes at that girl.

"Well, if it's so dumb, then you must know the answer. Right, May?" I said. "And so what *does* the fairy do with the teeth? Huh? She doesn't pay money just to throw them away, does she?"

After that, I waited and waited for her to answer.

The other children waited, too.

But May didn't say anything.

"Well?" I said.

"Well?" said Shirley.

"Well?" said José.

Finally, May's face turned red. And she went to get a drink of water.

After that, the whole lunch table started talking about the fairy. Only no one knew what she did with the teeth.

We wondered and wondered.

Then, all of a sudden, Lucille stood up.

And she fluffed her fluffy dress.

"Well, guess what? I don't really *care* what the tooth fairy does with the teeth. All I care about is how much money she leaves."

She looked at Room One. "You're nothing without money, people. Remember that," she said.

I tapped my fingers on the table kind of annoyed.

"Yeah, only that doesn't even answer my question, Lucille. 'Cause I still don't know what she does with the teeth."

Lucille put her hands on her hips.

"Well, maybe she just *collects* them," she said. "Did you ever think of that? Huh? Collecting stuff is a hobby, you know. My richie nana collects tons of junk. And she pays good money for it, too."

I tapped my fingers some more.

Then I put my chin in my hands. And I thought about Lucille's nana.

Finally, I started to smile a little bit. 'Cause maybe Lucille's idea might make some sense, possibly.

Pretty soon, Herb smiled a little bit, too.

"A *tooth* collection, huh?" he said. "Hmm. Maybe that's the answer, Junie B. Yeah, that just might be it. The fairy might collect teeth as a hobby or something."

"Sure," said Lennie. "There's nothing wrong with collecting stuff. Like, I collect baseball cards. But I don't really *do* anything with them."

"Sí, and I collect matchbox cars," said José. "What's wrong with that?"

Just then, Sheldon springed up from the table.

"Yes! And I collect vacuum-cleaner bags! And the doctor says that's perfectly normal!"

After that, Sheldon laughed. And he pretended to vacuum his pants.

All of us moved away from him.

Then the bell rang and everyone went outside for recess.

That afternoon, I wrote in my journal.

Dear first-grade journal,
 Me and Herb talked some more on the playground. We decided that the tooth fairy has a tooth ~~colekshun~~ collection, probably. And that is not even ~~werd~~ weird, possibly.

Also I promised Herb I would put my tooth under my pillow tonight.

I hope we are right about this woman.

From,

Junie B., First Grader

P.S. I wish me all the best.

9

Miracles!

That night, Mother put me in bed.

Daddy was in baby Ollie's room. He was trying to rock that cranky boy to sleep.

We heard Ollie fussing.

"I bet you're glad I'm not that bad. Right, Mother?" I said. "That baby is a pain in our necks. Right?"

Mother laughed. "Oh, believe me, Junie B., you were no peach when you were teething, either," she said.

She tickled me a little bit. "Speaking of teeth . . . tonight's the big night, right?"

she said. "Tonight's the night you're finally leaving your tooth for the fairy."

I covered my face with my sheet.

"Don't remind me," I said.

Mother laughed again. "Don't be silly. This is going to be fun."

She handed me my tooth to put under my pillow.

I handed it right back to her.

"You do it, Mother. You put it under my pillow, okay?" I said. "And put it close to the edge, please. 'Cause I don't want the fairy tramping around down there."

Mother put it close to the edge. She let me check it.

After that, she leaned down. And she gave me a big hug.

"I'm very proud of you, Junie B.," she said. "I'm proud that you got over all that silly nonsense Paulie Allen Puffer told you."

"Thank you," I said. "I am proud of me, too."

After that, Mother kissed me good night. And she turned out my light.

I quick turned it on again.

"Yeah, only I think I will sleep with the light on tonight," I said. "You know . . . just in case I have to come running out of my room in the middle of the night because there's a witch in here."

Mother did a sigh.

"Whatever," she said.

After that, she gave me another hug. And she closed my door.

I jumped up and opened it again.

"Yeah, only I think I will sleep with the door opened tonight," I said. "You know . . . just in case I start screaming my head off in the middle of the night because there's a witch in here."

Mother said, *"I give up."*

I give up means the same as *whatever,* I believe.

After that, she kissed me one more time.

And she left my room.

The next morning, I woke up very relieved.

Because guess what?

I made it through the night! That's what!

I hugged myself real happy.

Then, all of a sudden, I remembered about the fairy. And my heart started to pound and pound. 'Cause maybe there was money under my pillow right that very minute!

I took a big breath.

Then, very careful, I reached under

there. And I felt all around.
　　And bingo!
　　My fingers touched something!
　　I grabbed ahold of it and pulled it out.
　　Then I sat up straight in bed.
　　And I laughed and laughed.
　　'Cause good news! Ha!
　　CASH!

* * *

I zoomed to the kitchen and skipped around the table.

"CASH! CASH! I GOT CASH!" I hollered real thrilled.

"WHO WANTS TO SEE IT? HUH? WHO WANTS TO SEE MY CASH? PLEASE RAISE YOUR HANDS!"

I looked all around the kitchen.

Then I stopped skipping.

Because no one was actually in there.

I zoomed back down the hall.

"MOTHER! DADDY! WHERE ARE YOU? WHERE ARE YOU? THE FAIRY LEFT ME MONEY!"

Mother stuck her head out of Ollie's room. "We're in here, honey!" she called.

I skipped into Ollie's room and showed them my money.

"Look, people! I got cash! I got cash!" I said. "Only I don't know how much it adds up to. But it is a bundle, I bet!"

Daddy's eyes got big and wide at my money.

"Whoa! The tooth fairy must have been feeling very generous last night," he said.

"I know it," I said. "I love that fairy, Daddy. She left me money. And she didn't even pinch my cheeks!"

Ollie was sitting in his crib. He smiled out the bars at me.

I looked surprised at him.

"What's wrong with Ollie, Mother?" I asked. "Why is he smiling? Is he sick or something?"

Mother laughed. "No, silly," she said. "When I came in this morning, he was playing in his crib . . . happy as can be."

I scratched my head. "Really? Ollie's *happy*?" I said. "That's odd."

Daddy picked him up.

"Well, actually Ollie had a little surprise for us this morning, too," he said.

He sat down with Ollie on the floor. Then, very gentle, he took my finger. And he rubbed it against Ollie's gums.

"Hey!" I said. "It's *ridgedy*!"

Daddy grinned. "It sure is," he said. "That's Ollie's first tooth, Junie B."

My whole mouth came open at that good news!

"A *tooth*?" I said. "Ollie got a tooth?"

I felt the ridges some more.

"Wowie wow wow! Last night was a good tooth night for *both* of us!" I said.

"Yes, it was," said Daddy. "What a neat coincidence, huh? Ollie got his first tooth

on the very same night that the fairy came to get yours."

Mother ruffled my hair. "It's almost like Ollie was waiting for the tooth fairy to come, too, Junie B. Just like you."

I smiled at the thought of that.

Then, all of a sudden, I stood real still.

And goose bumps came on my arms.

"Wait a minute," I said real soft. "*What* did you just say, Mother?"

Mother looked at me kind of strange. "I said it's almost like Ollie was waiting for the tooth fairy to come, too."

Just then, I did a loud gasp.

"That's *it*!" I said. "That's *it*! That's *it*!"

I springed way high in the air. Then I twirled all around. And I hugged Mother real tight.

"Ollie *did* wait for the fairy!" I said. "He waited for the fairy, just like me!"

Mother and Daddy raised their eyebrows very curious.

I skipped all around them in a circle.

"Don't you *get* it?" I said. "The fairy *recycled*! She *recycled* my baby tooth! And she gave it to Ollie!"

My feet started to dance.

"It's perfect!" I said. "It's just like Dan, Dan the Soda Can! The fairy took my tooth! And she made it all shiny and new! And then she gave it to my very own baby brother!"

I quick bent down and felt Ollie's gum again.

"Yes-sir-ee-bob! That's my tooth, all right! I'd know that tooth anywhere!" I said.

Daddy scratched his head.

"Well, I'll be," he said.

Mother laughed. "What a great idea."

"It *is*, Mother!" I said. "It *is* a great idea! Plus also, it is a big relief. 'Cause the tooth fairy doesn't just throw teeth in the garbage. Now I know that for *sure*."

I looked at my money again.

"It's just like Miss Chris told us!" I said real squealy. "Recycling makes *cents*! Get it, Mother? Get it, Daddy? *Cents* sounds like *sense*! Ha! That's a good one, right?"

After that, I zoomed to my room to get dressed for school.

"I CAN'T WAIT TO TELL THE CHILDREN!" I hollered. "ROOM ONE IS GOING TO LOVE THIS NEWS!"

I put on my favorite pants and sweater.

Then I quick ran back to Ollie. And I felt his tooth some more.

He smiled at me some more.

I smiled back at him.

'Cause what do you know?

I think I might like that boy after all!

BARBARA PARK is one of today's funniest, most popular authors. Her middle-grade novels, which include *Skinnybones, The Kid in the Red Jacket, My Mother Got Married (And Other Disasters),* and *Mick Harte Was Here,* have won over forty children's book awards. Barbara holds a B.S. in education from the University of Alabama. She has two grown sons and lives with her husband, Richard, in Arizona.

DENISE BRUNKUS'S entertaining illustrations have appeared in over fifty books. She lives in New Jersey with her husband and daughter.